# Where the Root Rots

*Anne WestWood*

**ISBN-13:** *979-8-218-85331-0*

# Table of Contents

## Prologue

I still hear his voice sometimes—low, jagged, urgent—like barbed wire pulling through a throat.

"You have to hide."

That was all Ezra said.

Static hissed on the line, like breathing.

Then a shuffle, a grunt.

"Protect yourself, plea—"

Dead air.

I stayed there, phone pressed so hard to my ear it left a mark, listening to the emptiness as if he might claw his way back through it.

My hands shook so bad I nearly dropped the phone.

Later, I tried to convince myself I'd imagined it.

That the voice was wrong.

That the words weren't his.

But my chest still carried the echo—*you have to hide*—like a bruise that wouldn't heal.

That night in the woods, months ago—cold, dark, screaming—changed everything.

The night the man I had fallen for told me to run while he stayed behind, fighting his brother, saving my best friend.

The night the police and I returned to an empty campsite.

The night everyone vanished.

Sometimes I wonder if I'm crazy.

But the police believed the evidence, at least enough to search.

So it had to be real.

*Right?*

Since then, my life has shrunk to one thing: *research*.

Hours at my desk, digging into the Martin family.

Old clippings.

Mugshots.

Names that bled through Tennessee history like rust stains.

Their father's line traced back to the Chickamauga Cherokee, known as fierce, territorial, and relentless.

Newspaper scraps whispered of murders, stalking, assaults.

But none led to punishment.

Either the law couldn't reach them, or they scared off anyone who tried.

It's an old, twisted tale, and that violence runs in Graves' veins, shaping the monster inside him.

Evidence was scarce.

Scattered.

Questionable.

But I refused to stop until I found something—anything—that would bring Mara back.

Most days, the glow of the screen crawled under my skin like a parasite.

I cried over what might've been.

I rotted away in silence.

My therapist told me I need to "move on."

She thought it was like clinging to a high school breakup instead of a crime scene.

She didn't get it.

Nobody did.

"You're letting him win twice," she said once. "Once for what he did, and again every time you shut the world out."

I hated her for being right.

Because the truth is, I didn't have a safe place to spiral anymore.

Not since that night.

Not since Mara.

Not since Ezra.

And maybe that's why I was there—alone, contemplating returning to where it all started, asking myself the only questions that matter:

*What if I go back?*

*What if Graves is still out there?*

*What if I'm the only one who can bring them home?*

Nobody could convince me that returning wasn't right.

One night, I quickly packed my backpack and headed to the last place I had seen my best friend.

## Chapter 1: Preparation

The weight clanked against the floor like a drumbeat.

I was drenched in sweat, my lungs burning, and I didn't care.

I had to push harder.

The gym was empty, except for the hum of fluorescent lights and the occasional thud of a punching bag somewhere in the back.

I kept my eyes forward, fixed on nothing in particular, letting the rhythm of my movements drown out everything else.

I'd been running drills for what felt like hours.

Shadowboxing, sprints on the treadmill until my legs shook, rope jumps, squats with the heaviest dumbbells I could manage.

Every repetition, every drop of sweat, felt like a promise I was making to Mara.

She was out there somewhere, probably thinking I'd left her, thinking she was alone.

And she wasn't.

Not this time.

I hit the heavy bag again, my knuckles stinging from the impact.

The echoes in the empty gym bounced off the walls like ghosts, but I didn't care.

I was ready.

I had to be.

I paused and leaned against the bag, breathing hard, feeling my heartbeat pound in my chest.

I closed my eyes and saw her face: Mara, alone and afraid.

This image is how I fought my way through.

I couldn't and wouldn't fail her again.

Not ever.

I grabbed the jump rope again, wrapping it around my hands.

I moved to the center of the gym, circling like a predator, imagining the layout of the place I'd go back to.

I dropped into a series of push-ups, counting each one aloud even though there was no one to hear me.

"Thirty... thirty-one... thirty-two..." My arms burned, but I pushed further.

My legs trembled when I hit the wall for wall-sits.

My body was screaming at me to stop, but I ignored it.

Pain was temporary.

Saving Mara was forever.

After what felt like an eternity, I collapsed onto the mat, gasping, muscles trembling, sweat stinging my eyes.

I rolled onto my back, staring at the ceiling, and let myself feel it—the fear, the adrenaline, the drive that had been building since the moment I'd heard her scream the first time.

I could do this.

I *had* to do this.

My fingers flexed, curling like claws.

I thought about how I'd grab her, how I'd pull her free, how I'd fight every person who stood in the way.

I thought about her face when she would see me.

*Relief.*

Maybe even hope.

I swallowed hard.

I couldn't let her down.

I got up and headed toward the row of lockers.

I tossed my towel onto the bench and ran cold water over my face, letting it trickle down my neck, over my collarbones, soaking through the tank top I'd been wearing.

The chill made me shiver, but it also woke me up in a way nothing else could. I was now vigilant and awake.

The clock on the wall ticked relentlessly.

Every second brought me closer to her, and I wouldn't waste a single one.

I walked over to the punching bag again, wrapping my fists.

I hit it with everything I had, imagining the anger, the frustration, the fear being transferred into every punch.

This wasn't just training.

This was practice for survival—for both of us.

The first time had been messy, chaotic, almost too much to survive.

But I'd learned.

I've adapted.

By the time I stopped, my knuckles were raw, my arms shook with exhaustion, and I could barely catch my breath.

I stepped back and looked at myself in the mirror across the room.

Sweat dripped down my face, my hair stuck to my forehead in dark tangles.

My eyes were bright, hard.

Determined.

I clenched my fists.

I didn't need a weapon this time.

I was the weapon.

Every muscle in my body, every movement I'd honed, every ounce of will I had—it was all mine.

I gathered my things slowly, feeling my heartbeat calm.

The anticipation was there, but it was controlled now, tempered by preparation.

And this time, I wouldn't just be strong enough—I'd be *unstoppable*.

As I stepped out of the gym, the night air hit me like a slap.

The city was asleep, quiet and dark.

My boots hit the pavement, steady and confident.

17

I walked toward the car, toward the road that would take me back to the place I knew I shouldn't go—but had to.

Every streetlight, every shadow along the sidewalk felt like a warning, and I ignored it.

I had Mara waiting.

I had a second chance.

And I wouldn't waste it.

I slid into the driver's seat and started the engine.

The hum of the car sounded like the beginning of something inevitable.

My fingers tightened around the steering wheel.

I was going back.

And no one was going to stop me.

## Chapter 2: Pulled Back

The drive was off, unsettling.

Something didn't sit right, but I couldn't place what—except that I was heading straight into the Great Smoky Mountain National Park.

The sky was colorless—like someone had scraped the blue away and left only a gray smear.

The clouds hung low, thick and heavy, almost tangible.

I could've reached out the window and brushed them.

Fog wove between the trees, curling along the road, swallowing the mountains, hiding what waited ahead.

It set the tone for the trip, and I hated it.

I dreaded it.

But despite the dread, there was a pull I couldn't resist—an ache to find Mara.

Maybe Ezra, too.

My stomach twisted at the thought of confronting my demons: the haunted forest, the jagged mountains, and that monster, Graves.

A sudden gust rattled the windows, and for a heartbeat, I swore I saw a shadow move in the fog.

My pulse jumped.

It was probably nothing.

*But what if it wasn't?*

I caught a glimpse of the mountains through the mist, and it reminded me of when Mara and I first arrived here over a year ago.

I'd teased her for being glued to her phone instead of looking at the view.

Now I would've given anything to see her there, tapping and scrolling, oblivious of what was to come.

Nothing truly describes the pain of losing your best friend and then not knowing what became of her.

It rips you open from the inside out.

Tears welled, hot and unwelcome.

I tried the grounding exercise my therapist had taught me a few weeks prior.

*Why not give it a shot*, I thought.

Five things I can see: the cracked pavement, the ominous sky, the creeping fog, the twisted mountains, and my dashboard.

Four things I can touch: the leather steering wheel, my cold thigh, the hard plastic of the car door, and the leather on the console.

Three things I can hear: the Lumineers song playing softly, traffic humming by, wind whispering through the cracked windows.

Two things I can smell: my black-ice air freshener, the wintergreen gum I'd been chewing the whole drive.

One thing I can taste: revenge, bitter and sharp against my tongue.

Slowly, I calmed—or as calm as I could get—and the park entrance appeared through the haze.

The wooden sign swung slightly in the wind, weathered and crooked, the letters half-faded. My chest tightened, a fire sparking inside me.

I was on the hunt.

Mara.

Graves.

It didn't matter who I found first—I had five hours until sunset, and no time to waste.

The road narrowed, trees looming like silent sentinels.

Every snapping branch and rustling in the brush made me flinch.

My heart was hammering; I could hear it, feel it through all my limbs.

The forest felt alive—watching and waiting… for me.

And somewhere in that creeping fog, I knew Graves was out there.

I could feel his ghost-like presence.

And I would find him.

And I would bring Mara home.

* * *

I eased the car into a parking spot near the campsite marker, the tires crunching over gravel that seemed unnaturally loud in the emptiness.

The fog curled around the metal posts and picnic tables like it was haunted, slow-moving fingers.

The wooden signs and structures creaked in the wind.

The markers' faded letters were barely readable.

Rust covered the bolts, and graffiti covered the nearby picnic area.

Even the benches looked abandoned on purpose, as if no one wanted to be here.

*Why?*

I killed the engine.

The sudden silence pressed against my ears.

Wind shifted, snapping branches off trees and ripping the colorful fall leaves away.

A twig cracked somewhere just beyond the lot, not like the sound of the branches snapping from the trees.

I jumped at the sound.

*I wasn't alone.*

But I expected this.

I knew he wouldn't leave me alone.

I grabbed my backpack from the passenger seat, the strap scraping against my jacket.

My fingers trembled a little—from the cold or nerves, I couldn't tell.

The smell of the damp earth hit me like a slap to the face as I stepped further into the woods.

It was stronger than I remembered: moss, wet leaves, and something sharp, metallic.

The smell made my stomach tighten.

I took a slow, careful look around, then a small step forward.

The trail vanished into a wall of fog.

The place felt wrong, like the mountains themselves were holding their breath.

I forced myself to take another step.

The gravel crunched under me.

Suddenly, another crack shouted at me, closer this time.

I froze.

The wind whispered through the trees, carrying a sound that could have been anything—or anyone.

The forest waited.

Yet I was walking straight into it.

## Chapter 3: Traces

The fog hadn't lifted by morning.

It draped over the forest like a gray boundary, sucking in the trees and everything else along with it.

I hadn't closed my eyes all night; they were burning.

My body was stiff from spending the night in the car.

I decided to sleep in there rather than the tent, because at least it locks.

I crawled into the back and created a makeshift bed with my blankets and pillows.

But I couldn't stop thinking; my mind wouldn't stop racing.

About Mara.

About Ezra.

About Graves.

Every shadow in the fog looked like it was moving.

Breathing.

Waiting.

*Watching.*

I could feel the forest daring me to step inside, calling my name, testing me.

So I began reluctantly stepping.

I had to; there were no excuses.

The leaves underneath crunched against my hiking boots.

I weaved through all the different possible pathways of the trail.

Anxiety overwhelmed me, taking over all of me.

It was hard to understand how claustrophobic one can get in one of the biggest areas.

But Graves' eerie presence lurked everywhere in these mountains.

From the time I entered the foggy mountains in my car, I could feel his wraith.

I searched every inch of the second trail.

It was a dirt path with trees lining both sides.

It smelled like fresh pines, and it was refreshing to see such vibrant colors while on the hunt.

I had been inspecting the area for clues and signs for about three hours, searching for anything that proved Mara was alive.

And just when I started to give up, I noticed a fresh set of footsteps in a side path off the main trail.

I followed the prints all the way till they stopped, which led to a small pond.

It was barely big enough to be anything else besides land.

However, it led to my first clue: Mara's necklace.

We bought matching ones during our freshman year of high school.

Hers has a rose pendant and is gold, mine has a daisy pendant and is silver.

And there was hers, barely hanging from a limp branch.

It hung there, delicate and innocent… but the placement screamed like a warning.

It was almost perfectly placed.

*Was I hunting for the prey?*

*Or was I the prey?*

I grabbed the necklace and made a run for my car.

I didn't look back.

Forward was the only way.

My legs felt like jello, and my lungs were burning like I'd taken shots of Fireball.

I ran as if my life depended on it—like the night I escaped whatever truly happened.

I quickly and clumsily jumped into my vehicle, locked the doors, and nervously checked the area.

Nothing was near.

It could've been my imagination, but once you're in those woods for so long, your mind plays tricks on you.

I held the necklace up close and checked it.

It was Mara's rose necklace, no doubt; definitely hers.

*But why was it there, and why was it placed like that?*

*Could it have gotten caught while she was running?*

*Was it a coincidence that I found it?*

My mind was spinning.

**Knock.**

**Knock.**

**Knock.**

I jumped at the sound, my heart stopped for a second, and my stomach twisted painfully.

I looked up in fright.

A man, older… no clue who he was.

But he had impeccably bad timing.

I hardly rolled my window down, "Hello?"

"Hey. I saw you sprinting from the trail. Is everything okay?"

"Oh, yes. Thank you."

But he didn't walk away.

We stared awkwardly at each other till he finally continued, "Why were you running?"

"Oh, just a, uh, bear."

"Damn. Thanks for telling me, I don't do bears."

"Yeah," I awkwardly chuckled and rolled my window up.

He lingered around the car, the parking lot, the trail, but eventually I lost track of him, and he had vanished.

There might've been a clue about Mara, but I had to get out of there.

So, I moved to the spot where I knew there would be a clue: *the willow tree.*

## Chapter 4: Rotten Secrets

I hopped out of the car as soon as I pulled up to the path leading to the willow.

It had been so long since I had seen it.

I loved that tree—or maybe it was the memories it held.

Either way, it was special to me.

I jogged toward the clearing where Ezra and I once laughed, danced, ran, and loved.

But the once breathtaking sanctuary, with its swaying branches and soft green canopy, had turned into a ruin.

The willow was hacked near the trunk, deep gouges like a chainsaw's bite.

I stared at the splintered wood, my knees buckling as I dropped to the ground.

It wasn't the tree itself that crushed me—it was what it meant.

Everything special in my life seemed to collapse in the end.

My mom.

My dad.

Mara, our friendship.

Ezra, or who I thought he was.

Now this damn willow tree.

The willow's rotting trunk's sour and damp odor filled my nose.

Something that was once so beautiful was now wasting away.

I scrambled at the roots, searching for Ezra's hidden box—the one where he'd stashed clues, the blankets, the pieces of us.

But all I found was a hole in the dirt where it used to be.

This place had been destroyed, and it felt like a *personal attack.*

It had Graves' name written all over it.

I sat on one of the fallen limbs, stroking the torn bark.

The roughness bit into my palm until I felt something else—something carved.

I leaned closer: M-A-R.

My nickname for Mara.

*Was this a sign?*

*Did she leave it for me?*

*How long had it been there?*

I snapped a picture, heart hammering, and forced myself up.

If this place were gone, then my only option would be forward.

Ezra had always talked about the cabin being nearby, in some hidden spot.

I had to find it.

A narrow path split off the main clearing, half-hidden by brush.

I followed it to an irregularly large oak tree.

*Left or right?*

*Right.*

The path grew rough, roots and rocks tangling beneath my boots.

The tree limbs cover the sky, painting a nice yellow shade.

Thirty minutes later, scratched and sweating, I finally stumbled onto a shack.

Not a cabin exactly—but something.

More than I'd seen in an hour.

I circled the building carefully.

The earth sloped down to a small door at the bottom—a basement.

Maybe this was the "cabin" Ezra had mentioned.

I didn't know what to trust anymore—not with the Martin brothers.

"You're a busy little lady."

The voice behind me snapped my spine straight.

My stomach knotted.

I knew that voice—the man from my car window.

I didn't stop walking.

"Yes. Getting in all the hikes," I said, trying to sound casual.

"I can see that," he said. "But how'd you get all the way out here?"

I gave a strained laugh. "Same way as you."

He paused. "Well, you see…"

I cut in. "I really have to keep going. I'm on a mission to hit 10,000 steps today."

"Well, that's my path," he said quickly and unsettlingly.

"These are all mine—my sons and I use them to get to our spots on our land. It's not open to the public."

I swallowed hard.

"I'm so sorry, sir. I didn't realize. I'll get off your property right now."

"Well, now."

He smiled without warmth. "I'll let it slide. Don't get upset. You've had a rough day already—with that bear and all."

A half-smile was all I could manage.

He was giving me emotional whiplash—his tone flipping from casual to threatening within seconds.

"Want to join me for a beer?" he asked.

"No, thank you. Like I said, I have my step goal."

"Come on. Have a beer."

He seemed insistent; it made me even more uneasy.

"No, thank you, sir. But I appreciate the offer."

I started toward him, aiming to pass and get the hell out of there.

As I did, I forced a polite smile. "It was very nice to meet you."

He gave me a grin then—chilling, haunting.

The same smile I'd seen on Graves.

That's when it clicked.

The "sons."

The odd behavior.

The sinister smile.

This wasn't just some hiker who happened to live on land near the park.

This was *Dennis Martin*.

## Chapter 5: Oh No

As soon as I hit the main trail, I ran.

Not jogged—ran.

Sprinting hard enough that my lungs and legs felt like fire.

My mind couldn't process what had just happened—standing face-to-face with the very man Ezra had warned me about.

Dennis Martin wasn't a story.

He wasn't a name buried in the newsprint.

He was here.

In these woods.

And now he knew I was too.

All that made sense was that danger was near.

I was being watched.

Hunted.

I wasn't alone out here.

If Dennis was lurking, Graves couldn't be far behind—maybe even walking right beside him, hidden in the shadows, the way Graves always is.

The path was empty.

Not a single bystander.

No hikers.

Nothing.

The sky pressed low and dark, clouds hanging over the trees like a lid.

Roots clawed up through the dirt, grabbing at my boots like snares with every stride.

And then I noticed it—*the quiet.*

It was too quiet.

A whistle drifted through the distance, sharp and thin.

Almost as if it were summoning me back to the danger.

Dennis?

Graves?

I didn't wait to find out.

I pushed harder, my heart punching my ribs, using every ounce of strength to reach the parking lot.

When I finally broke through the tree line into the parking lot, winded and limp, a man appeared in front of me, propped against the back of a truck.

His back was to me.

He glanced over his shoulder—just enough for me to see a shadow of his face under the brim of his baseball cap.

Those lips.

Those eyes—even hidden, I knew them.

*Ezra.*

I froze mid-step.

My throat closed around his name.

*Should I call out?*

*Run to him?*

*Leave him alone?*

I opened my mouth, but the word caught, and died.

By the time I reached my car and looked back, both he and the truck were gone.

Vanished, like I had only dreamt them from my imagination.

I locked the doors and sat there, face in hands, head pounding, heart skipping beats.

Memories poured in, drowning me:

Ezra's easy laugh.

His warm, calloused hands.

The way we whispered in the tent until we fell asleep, our breath colliding.

His lips on my neck.

The way my stomach fluttered under his gaze.

The way he made me feel like the only girl who mattered.

For a moment, I let it happen.

I closed my eyes and let the tears spill hot and uncontrolled, carving salt trails down my cheeks.

I hadn't cried like that in months.

Maybe I *needed* to.

Suddenly, an engine roared behind me, making me jump.

My eyes shot to the rearview mirror.

That blue truck was back.

I slid down in my seat, heart pounding so hard it made my vision pulse.

I watched through the side-view mirror as the door swung open and a pair of heavy military boots hit the gravel.

"Oh no," I whispered to no one.

"No, no, no…"

That wasn't *Ezra*.

It was *Graves*.

## Chapter 6: Gravel Road

I couldn't do much after that.

I was too stunned by the realization.

So I drove a good way away, locked the doors, and crawled into the back, wasting the hours.

Rain hammered the roof while I sat in the dark, music blaring, trying to drown out my thoughts.

* * *

I woke to the roar of a pickup rattling past.

Blue.

Rusty.

Maybe the same Martins' truck.

I bolted upright, fumbled for the keys, and followed.

The truck wove through the Smoky Mountains, each curve pulling me deeper into the wilderness.

Then its turn signal blinked.

Slowly, hesitantly, patiently.

A narrow gravel road appeared, flanked by pines.

I knew better than to follow down a road like that.

So I kept going, catching just enough of a glimpse to confirm what I had feared—Dennis was driving.

My stomach turned.

Something about him, about Graves, about all of it… was *wrong*.

And Mara was tangled right in the middle of it.

I pulled off a few miles down, engine off, and pretended to "break down" while rain streaked the glass.

I traced routes on the park map, pretending to plan, though my thoughts circled only one thing.

Then—taillights hit my mirror.

I ducked low, breath cut.

The truck rumbled past, rounding the bend ahead.

This was my chance.

I spun the key, whipped a U-turn, and darted onto the gravel road.

It stretched on for miles, gravel fading to dirt, dirt thinning until the woods pressed close on either side.

At last, I reached a clearing.

Tire tracks circled the space like a crude parking lot.

I stepped out, heart pounding, and followed a narrow path into the trees.

Every rustle made me twitch.

Every shadow pulled my gaze.

I walked down the old trail.

Pine filled my nostrils, and my eyes began to itch.

Finally, the cabin appeared—the same one I had stumbled upon before.

Dark.

Still.

Eerie.

No vehicles outside, right now.

Vacant, or staged.

I crouched low, listening.

*Nothing.*

I struggle internally, battling with my own thoughts.

*Is this right?*

*Is this okay?*

*This is my only shot.*

I sprinted to the nearest window.

Unlocked.

Too easy.

A gift—or a trap.

I slipped inside.

The air was stale.

Books on the table. Reading glasses. A comb. The musk of men's cologne. One of the Martin brothers' rooms.

I searched the room, and I had a feeling it was Ezra's, and I was right.

My foot snagged on a loose board. As I bent to steady myself, I saw a new journal wedged beneath it.

I grabbed it, stuffed it in my bag, and didn't look back.

I crept forward, crawling, pausing at every sound.

I peered through the crack: a hallway.

Another door across, and one to the left.

My hands trembled on the knob.

I forced myself to breathe, then pushed it open.

The hinges groaned—*krkrk.*

I froze.

*Silence.*

Then I slid through and into the room on the left.

*The Bathroom.*

I tore through drawers, the hamper, and the shower curtain.

*Nothing.*

Four toothbrushes sat in a cup—black, gray, red… and purple.

*Mara's?*

*Or just a coincidence?*

The mirror caught me.

Its edge bulged oddly.

*A hidden cabinet.*

Inside: a pink hairbrush, the same style Mara once carried.

Shampoo. Conditioner. Women's body wash.

My mind spun.

*If no woman has ever lived here, then why are these items here?*

*And if Mara was captive, why care for her?*

I slipped back out, heart racing, and crossed to the last door.

I opened it—and froze.

*Mara.*

Unconscious.

Shackled to the bed, wrists cuffed raw.

Her bones showed through against her pale skin, her mouth sealed with duct tape.

The stench of urine filled the room.

I rushed to her, tears blurring my sight.

"Mara," I whispered, kneeling close. "Mara."

*No answer.*

I pressed my trembling fingers to her throat—weak, but alive.

Relief buckled my knees.

I searched for keys, anything to break her free—

Then the rumble came.

An *engine*.

Angry, fast, growing louder.

No time.

If I stayed, neither of us would make it out.

Choking on tears, I squeezed her hand.

"I'll come back, I promise," I whispered.

Then I tore myself away, climbed through the window, and vanished into the stormy forest with my bag stuffed full of evidence.

## Chapter 7: Too Close

I didn't realize how close they were.

I should've waited instead of running, but I had no choice.

All I could do was get out of there.

Dennis and Graves were together in the pickup, barreling between trees, searching for me.

I sprinted toward the direction of my car, praying under my breath that I wouldn't get caught.

Limbs whipped against my arms and face as the gloomy sky bled into night.

My legs burned.

My body was numb.

I was cold, soaked, and trembling.

The outline of the "parking lot" appeared through the trees.

I tripped, sliding hard on mud, catching myself against a rock, and ducking behind it for protection.

The truck's rumble had gone silent.

They were waiting for me—I could feel it.

A few seconds later, a voice ripped through the quiet.

"JOR-DYYY!"

*Graves.*

"WHERE ARE YOUUUU?"

His voice echoed again, thin and sharp, piercing my ears and churning my stomach.

I'd seen what he'd done to Mara.

And I knew what he would do to me.

Leaves crunched somewhere in the distance—thankfully not close… yet.

I curled myself into a ball, holding my breath.

My thoughts spun, but no plan came.

Only stillness.

Then a horn shattered the silence.

One long, furious wail, echoing through the trees.

I jumped at the sound of it.

"Let's go!" Dennis shouted.

"But she's still out here," Graves snapped back.

"We'll get her next time. She'll be back."

Their voices faded into muffled yelling.

Graves didn't want to leave.

I stayed frozen, counting seconds, until the truck's engine roared and finally sped off.

I waited minutes, hours more like, before daring to crawl to my knees.

I could *not* get caught.

*Not now.*

At last, I crept to my car, unlocking it and darting for the nearest passenger door. I slid inside and locked it, crouching low.

That's when I saw him—*Graves*—staring at me through the windshield.

My stomach lurched at the sight of his wicked smile.

My fingers fumbled with the keys, clumsy and frantic, before jamming them into the ignition.

I slammed the car into reverse and ripped away.

Graves remained, a dark figure in the rain.

That was too close.

Way too close.

But at least I was *alive*.

At least I was *free*.

## Chapter 8: Captive

*Flashback: Mara's Story*

I never imagined that a simple camping trip would end with me trapped in someone else's twisted world.

I guess that's what I get for being too trusting, too open, too admiring.

Maybe I should've known better.

I still don't understand Graves's obsession.

All I know is I wish it had never begun.

Now he keeps me in a basement, locked inside a cold, damp room.

The air smells faintly of mold and something worse I can't quite name.

Once a week, he brings me food.

Two bottles of water to last me until the next time.

That's all I get.

I'm starving.

I've lost nearly fifteen pounds.

My ribs stick out more each day.

My skin is pale, almost translucent under the dim light from the single bulb above me.

At the beginning, he didn't keep me in chains like he does now.

At least I had some freedom to move, though it didn't feel like it.

But that's my fault.

He told me so.

I should've obeyed him—and Dennis too.

Instead, I plotted against them.

I waited until Graves was vulnerable and I struck.

That was my one victory, though Dennis told me it made me more devil than angel.

He knew the Bible like the back of his hand and used it like a weapon, twisting every story, every passage, to justify his words and actions.

I trusted Dennis.

I believed I could rely on him.

He reminded me of my father.

Calm.

Predictable.

The kind of man who made you feel safe.

He was even the one who got me moved to this room, this place I now call my cage.

At first, I had my own bedroom.

No chains.

No men.

I could write in my notebook, listen to records, and watch old black-and-white TV shows that made me forget where I was for a few precious hours.

I tried to fill the emptiness with small routines, little bits of normalcy, because that's all I had left.

I didn't mind it at first.

But that's also when I began to lose hope that anyone was coming for me.

I didn't know what had happened to Jordy.

Graves wouldn't let Ezra see me anymore.

Ezra became the errand boy, the clean-up boy, the one who obeyed every command without question.

Graves's words, not mine.

Graves even told me he wanted to kill Ezra, just like he did Talon—but his father wouldn't allow it.

Then one day, something inside Graves snapped.

A switch flipped.

He no longer wanted me free, and I knew it instantly, long before the chains clamped around my wrists and ankles.

He stormed into my room abruptly and angrily, yet not saying a single word.

His footsteps were like knives on the floor.

Without warning, he shoved me onto the bed.

Cold metal instantly clamped around my wrists, biting my skin, and shackles locked my ankles in place.

*Everything* changed after that.

Showers once a week.

One bathroom break.

No outlets.

No sunlight.

Just a room, a bed, and my own mind.

And that might have been the cruelest torture of all—my thoughts eating at me, gnawing day after day, night after night.

So I slept.

I slept every second of every day until my body became numb, until the hours blurred together and I felt like a ghost of myself.

But in all the time I've been here, I never remembered a dream.

Not until last night.

It was Jordy, whispering in my ear.

It felt so real that I wanted to reach out and touch her.

I could almost feel her lips brushing my ears.

She promised she would come back.

I wanted to believe her so badly.

I missed her more than I could ever describe.

I missed my parents, my house, the smell of rain on the driveway, and the way the morning sunlight hit my bedroom window.

I missed the person I used to be.

Even if I escape someday, I know I'll never be the same again.

Something inside me has shifted, cracked, warped.

But I will survive.

I will persevere.

I just have to get out of here first.

I just have to find the strength to fight, to outsmart, to *live*.

And hope Jordy *really* does come back for me.

## Chapter 9: Whispered Words

I couldn't get the image of Mara out of my head—sickly skinny, chained to the bed, alone in that dark room.

It killed me to think about how long she'd been trapped like that.

But I kept driving—mile after mile—until the twisting roads and thickening fog told me I was far enough away to breathe again.

I ended up in Zion Grove, a quiet mountain town wedged between ridges that rolled like waves.

I pulled onto a dirt sliver off the main road near Bird Creek and parked.

For the first time in hours: silence.

No tires on gravel.

No heavy breathing.

Just wind and water.

The second I threw the car into park, I reached for the journal I'd found at the house.

It was creased and damp at the corners, the spine cracked from his restless hands.

I flipped to the first page: *Ezra Martin.*

Page after page—his handwriting, familiar, jagged, impatient.

It was like touching him again, hearing him again, through the way his words curved and bled into one another.

His entries began:

January 2025

*I've finally managed to manipulate Graves enough to earn some freedom.*

*I've agreed to be his errand-boy, earning respect for doing the small things.*

*He thinks he has control over me—that was my goal all along.*

*I will never forgive him for what he's done to Talon, to Mara, even to Jordy.*

*Thankfully, he's given up on Jordy... for now.*

*But he isn't good to Mara; I'm worried about her.*

*I'm not allowed to speak, or even be in the same room as her, but I can hear her crying.*

*I see the "plates" and water they take to her.*

*It's not fair.*

*She doesn't deserve this.*

*But as of now, I can't think of a way to get us out.*

*Graves has Dennis on his side, and that's even scarier than Graves alone.*

*Dennis is smart, calculating, and vengeful.*

*My one job for now is to play along, so that's exactly what I'll do.*

February 2025

*The walls are tightening.*

*Every day, the leash gets shorter.*

*Graves keeps sending me into town, handing me small tasks and bits of money like rewards.*

*He thinks it's trust, but I know it's a test—he's watching to see if I'll run, if I'll slip.*

*I keep my face blank, my voice calm, my hands steady.*

*The taste of freedom feels like a trick.*

*Today I caught a glimpse of Mara.*

*Just a flicker through the door before Dennis closed it.*

*She's thinner now, her hair dull, her eyes glassy.*

*The crying has stopped—now there's only silence, and somehow that's worse.*

*I wanted to reach for her, but Dennis was leaning between us, watching.*

*Graves still thinks I'm his errand-boy.*

*Dennis doesn't.*

*I see it in his eyes; he's waiting for me to mess up.*

*I keep telling myself to smile, nod... survive.*

*But the anger's growing, splintering under my skin.*

*If I can't find a way out soon—if I can't get Mara out before she disappears completely—I don't know how much longer I can keep playing along.*

March 2025

*I don't get much time to write.*

*Dennis hovers, peeking over my shoulder, pretending to be casual, but I know what he's doing.*

*This notebook is the one thing that's mine—hidden under a loose board, written in fragments when no one's looking.*

*If they found it, it would be gone, or worse, used against me.*

*So I write fast, in stolen moments, like now.*

*I keep thinking about Jordy.*

*I don't even know where she is anymore.*

*I miss her voice, the way she used to look at me like I wasn't a monster.*

*When I close my eyes, I can almost feel her near me, like a memory that doesn't want to fade.*

*Graves says he's "done" with her, but I don't believe him.*

*Everything I care about is gone.*

*This is the only space that's still mine—these words, these hidden lines— even if it's dangerous.*

*I tell myself to stay patient.*

*Play along.*

*Smile when Graves calls me "son."*

*Act dumb when Dennis looks suspicious.*

*But I don't know how much longer I can keep this up.*

April 2025

*The balance in this house is shifting.*

*I can feel it in the way the air changes when Graves walks into a room.*

*He talks louder.*

*He fills the space like it belongs to him.*

*Even Dennis listens.*

*I never thought I'd see the day my father would take orders from my brother, but here we are.*

*Graves plays a dangerous game—soft-spoken one moment, sharp the next, always keeping us guessing.*

*I hate how good he's gotten at it.*

*Dennis is drinking more.*

*He mutters about being "disrespected," about how nobody listens to him anymore.*

*He's paranoid—thinks people are watching the house, that someone's coming for him.*

*Maybe he's right.*

*Maybe it's guilt eating him alive.*

*Either way, it makes him dangerous.*

*The drunker he gets, the quicker he turns.*

*I've been keeping my head down, pretending not to notice the cracks forming between them.*

*They don't realize how much I see, how much I remember.*

*Graves wants power, Dennis wants control, and I just want out.*

*This place doesn't belong to me anymore.*

*Not unless they're gone for good.*

May 2025

*Something in me is starting to splinter.*

*For months, I've been patient, playing along, letting Graves bark orders and Dennis track my every move.*

*I've smiled, nodded, taken the insults, and done the errands.*

*But the air in this house feels heavier now, pressing down on my chest.*

*I can't tell if it's them changing or me.*

*Dennis has gotten worse.*

*He's stopped pretending to be a father and started acting like a warden.*

*He counts the food, the hours I'm gone, and keeps track of everything.*

*If I'm five minutes late, he's waiting at the door.*

*Graves feeds off it—he enjoys watching Dennis lose control.*

*He enjoys watching me endure it.*

*So I've started hiding small things—matches, bandages, water under the floorboard where this notebook sleeps.*

*I rehearse what I'd do if I had to run, if I had to fight.*

*It's dangerous, even thinking about it.*

*But thinking is the only thing that keeps me steady.*

*Something is going to give.*

*Maybe them.*

*Maybe me.*

July 2025

*They caught me.*

*Not the dramatic kind you see in movies—no shouting, no sirens—but Dennis found the hidden supplies when he was drunk and nosy, the way he is when the bottle loosens him up.*

*He lifted the loose board because something in him wouldn't stop turning over the house.*

*Graves watched him pry it up with that quiet smile, like he already knew.*

*I should have known better.*

*I should have moved everything further away, deeper.*

*The only thing I saved was my journal, which I forgot to return to my hidden spot and left in the drawer of my nightstand.*

*Graves took my errands away, assigned me to the yard, to the cold work that keeps a man's hands raw and his head empty.*

*Dennis followed me around like a shadow, waiting for me to slip.*

*When I tried to write, there was always someone inside the house, humming, clearing their throat, pretending they needed something from me.*

*I moved my notebook back under the same board, but I'm writing in shorter bursts now, if at all.*

*This is harder than chains.*

*Graves said a lot of words that tasted like iron.*

*He told me I was ungrateful, useless, a child.*

*Dennis agreed, and his voice broke half the time, the way drunk men do when they try to sound fierce.*

*I swallowed every insult because I knew what happened when I didn't.*

*Jordy comes back to me in the quiet of the night, in dreams with possibility, and I wake up with a mouth full of salt.*

*If I'm caught like this—if I can't even breathe without them noticing—how will I get her back?*

*How will I get Mara out?*

*Even when they think they've taken everything—freedom, tools, time—they haven't taken my head.*

September 2025

*It's officially been a year.*

*A full damn year since everything fell apart—since the woods, since her.*

*Time feels different now.*

*Long and slow, like the walls are breathing with me, waiting for something to crack.*

*Dennis has been on edge again.*

*He's been going crazy because he thinks he saw someone near the tree line last night.*

*Said it was a girl—small, fast, moved like she knew where she was going.*

*He yelled for Graves, but by the time they got outside, whoever it was was gone.*

*They searched the property, cussing and stomping through the dark, but found nothing.*

*I stayed by the window, staring into the trees.*

*I didn't see anyone, but I felt her.*

*Graves said it was "kids snooping," but I don't buy that.*

*Dennis hasn't slept since.*

*He's been pacing, staking out the house, muttering about how someone's coming for us, and we're being watched.*

*He might be drunk, but I think—for once—he's right.*

*If it was her out there... I don't know what I'd do.*

*Run to her, or warn her to stay away.*

*I want to see her, to tell her the truth, but the truth would only put her in danger.*

*Graves is colder than ever.*

*He's planning something—something final.*

*If Jordy really came back to these woods, she needs to leave before he finds her.*

*Before it's too late.*

\* \* \*

I held my breath the whole time I was reading.

Each page felt like a confession meant for me—like he'd been talking straight through the pages, knowing one day I would hear him.

His handwriting was the same—slanted, restless—but the voice underneath it... It wasn't the Ezra I remembered.

He sounded tired.

Cornered.

Stuck.

I kept stopping to look up, half expecting him to be there, standing in front of my windshield, waiting for me.

I could feel him unraveling with every line.

He was trapped in that house, fighting ghosts that still breathe.

And all this time, I thought I was the only one haunted.

I don't know if finding this makes it better or worse.

He's warned me, but I've never been good at listening.

Because all I can think is—if he really is still out there…

Maybe I can save him, too.

## Chapter 10: He's Watching

I woke to a muffled ding coming from my phone.

It was strange; nobody should've been texting me.

*I had nobody to text.*

Apprehensive yet oddly hopeful, I reached for the phone.

"I know you're here."

That was all it said.

My heart dropped into my stomach, a heavy pit forming that sent panic rushing through me.

I couldn't breathe.

The anxiety hit before I realized what was happening.

My chest tightened first.

It was a slow, invisible fist closing around my lungs.

I couldn't pull in air no matter how hard I tried; it was like breathing through a straw.

My heart slammed against my ribs, too fast, too loud, each beat echoing in my ears until it drowned out everything else.

The room tilted.

My vision tunneled, edges going fuzzy, black creeping in like spilled ink.

My arms went numb, pins and needles stabbing up my skin.

*This is it,* I thought.

*I'm dying.*

I pressed a hand to my chest, desperate to slow my heart, but it only thrashed harder.

Time stretched and twisted until all I knew was fear and suffocation.

Then, just as suddenly, it began to break.

My heartbeat eased, shallow breaths turning deeper.

My fingers tingled as feeling returned.

I sat there shaking, drenched in sweat, trying to convince myself it was over.

*But it wasn't.*

The panic attack had passed.

Graves hadn't.

*What am I going to do?* I thought.

*Now that he's watching me like a hawk?*

I knew how good they were at that, from Ezra's journal I'd just read.

I locked the doors and started to make a plan.

A rescue plan.

A final plan to put an end to this once and for all.

The next day was the day I'd been waiting for this entire year.

The mission was in motion—day one of the end.

To save my best friend.

To save the love of my life.

I packed my gear: rope, binoculars, a knife, protein bars, and a water bottle.

I laced up my boots tightly and pulled my black hoodie over my wild ponytail.

Then I was gone, disappearing into the mountains, into the trees, into the beautiful wilderness that always felt dark and watchful.

It felt like the forest knew me.

The wind moved through the branches like whispering voices, like the trees were sharing my secrets.

I crawled beneath a fallen tree blocking the path, mud soaking through my leggings.

My pulse quickened; I could feel it… I was getting closer.

Just a little farther.

After a few more minutes, I reached the treeline surrounding the cabin.

I found a small hollow that looked like a deer den and claimed it as my hiding spot.

I pulled out my binoculars and began to watch.

The place appeared lived-in.

All I could hope was that Graves was in there—and not somewhere out here, watching me.

## Chapter 11: Stakeout

I'd been awake for nearly twenty-four hours.

My eyes felt heavy, my head spun, and little vertigo flickers that made the world tilt.

All night, I'd been seeing my mom and dad standing beside me, which wasn't possible.

*Hallucinations*, I told myself.

Exhaustion.

Still, I couldn't stop.

I couldn't delay.

I had to get Mara and Ezra out of there.

I'd decided to wait until I saw the truck leave with Dennis and Graves.

After that, it would be time.

For now, it was a waiting game.

My phone buzzed in my pocket—one buzz, then another. *Graves*, I thought, and pulled it out.

His text read:

"Checked on your car again… you're gone today…"

A second one followed:

"Where'd you go, Jordy?"

I turned my phone off and shoved it back into my pocket, forcing myself to keep watch.

I ran the logic over and over in my head: *Graves was gone now; he'd be looking for me. If Dennis left and Graves didn't return, I could slip into the cabin unnoticed.*

I tried not to think about him watching me sleep every morning.

I kept glancing over my shoulder, waiting for movement.

I was too exposed in the deer den.

It felt like a stage with no curtains.

I needed *true* cover.

I inspected the property and found the garage, a lean-to shop attached to the side of the house.

The doors were cracked and sagging, off their tracks in places, a thin strip of weeds separating them from the main building.

Impulse shoved me forward.

I ran.

I reached the doors and slid under the middle one, back scraping the concrete.

The shop smelled like oil, old rubber, and dead gasoline.

The floor was a patchwork of dark stains where people had tried—and failed—to clean up.

Tools crowded a battered bench; rags and jars of bolts collected grease like dust.

And on the wall, keys dangled—two sets, like the punchline to a joke.

A beat-up silver 2014 Ford F-150 sat beside a sun-faded '99 Toyota Camry.

Their keys swayed on the pegboard like a dare.

Everything shifted.

No more trudging through the woods with Mara and Ezra—we could drive out and be gone in minutes.

I snagged both sets, shoved them into my backpack, and dropped down on the cold floor to watch.

Hours crawled.

Finally, Dennis climbed into the blue pickup and pulled away, the truck's taillights shrinking until they vanished into the trees.

I counted a few more breaths, then moved… quickly.

Before I left the shop, I climbed into the F-150 and turned the key to check the gas level.

The engine coughed, then died—the battery was dead.

The Camry did the same cough, then roared to life.

The gas was near empty, but that was fine.

All I needed was enough gas to get me to my car.

I crawled out of the garage and darted for the nearest window.

It was unlocked—just like the last time.

I squeezed through into the living room, keeping low, and made my way down the hallway.

It led to the bedrooms of Mara and Ezra.

Mara's door was locked.

Someone had added a new deadbolt since the last time I'd been here.

No key.

I went to Ezra's door and found it unlocked.

The room smelled like old sweat and stale air.

Ezra sat on the edge of the bed, hollow-eyed and small, his wrists raw where metal had bitten him.

Cuts crusted his cheek; he looked like someone who'd been worn down to the last thread.

"Jordy?" His voice was a croak of confusion.

"Yes. It's me."

Relief flooded me—so sharp it made my stomach flutter, almost as if butterflies lived inside.

I grabbed his face in both hands. "I'm getting you out, right now. We have to move fast. Can you stand?"

He nodded slowly, still half-sedated. "Do you know where the keys are?"

The keys weren't anywhere in sight—Graves had taken them, of course.

I ripped through drawers, overturned a chair, kicked at the rug—nothing but dust and tools.

Then I spotted a shine under the workbench: a thin strip of wire, rusted and bent.

I pulled it free and worked it between my fingers until it formed a hook.

"Hold still," I whispered.

Ezra didn't argue.

His breath became shallow, eyes half-closed.

The cuffs had clawed his skin raw and crusted it with maroon blood.

My stomach churned, and I nearly vomited at the sight of them.

Despite the disturbing image, I steadied my hands and narrowed my eyes, focusing intently as if I had tunnel vision.

I slid the wire into the first cuff and turned, slow at first, then harder when it wouldn't catch.

Sweat slicked my palms; every scrape and creak sounded gigantic in the quiet room.

Then—click.

The metal surrendered.

The remaining cuff fought me like a live thing, but I worked faster, beating the lock with patience and force until it, too, released.

The chain hit the floor with a haunting clatter that echoed throughout the house.

Ezra collapsed forward into me, and I caught him in my arms.

His body was limp, as if he had no control over it.

For a long breath, we simply sat—his weight, the thud of his heart against mine, the air finally moving between us.

Relief hit like a truck, sudden and overwhelming.

I let myself breathe it for a second, and then the weight returned: *Mara*.

I still had to get her.

"Can you stand?" I asked, holding him up with my arms.

"Yes."

"Are you sure?"

He nodded.

"We need to grab Mara first, then we'll walk to the car. Do you know where they keep the key for Mara's room?"

"Check the bathroom," he said.

I ripped the medicine cabinet open and ransacked drawers.

However, I came up empty-handed.

"Not there," I yelled from the bathroom.

"Check above the door," he croaked.

His voice became softer as he spoke.

I stepped up on a stool and ran my hand along the doorframe until my fingers brushed a small brass key.

I grabbed it eagerly, treating it like a precious gift, and then I hesitantly inserted it into the lock.

The deadbolt put up a stubborn fight, refusing to budge at first.

But with a reluctant creak, it finally relented, releasing its grip with a slow sigh.

With a gentle twist of the knob, the door creaked open.

## Chapter 12: Salvation

The door breathed open like it was exhaling someone's soul.

The stench instantly burned my nose; a mixture of urine, mildew, chemicals, and sour must.

The stench was even more overwhelming than it had been previously; it even made it difficult to breathe.

She was withering away, trapped in the grip of life while her essence slowly faded.

Then, her eyes began to flicker.

I ran to her as Ezra kept watch.

The handcuffs and shackles restrained her.

And they added a rag to her mouth.

I glanced at her nightstand full of empty cups, prescription bottles, and needles.

I hadn't noticed it when I was here the first time.

*Were they drugging her?*

I cupped Mara's face after ripping out the rag.

"Mara, it's me, Jordy."

Her eyes were still closed, but she responded, "Are...are you real?"

"Yes, I am, and we have to hurry. We don't have much time, Mar."

She nodded her head, agreeing, yet her eyes remained shut.

"Mara, can you open your eyes?"

"No, too… tired."

"Can you walk?"

She coughed, then answered: "… not sure."

Ezra joined me and used a large pair of bolt cutters to remove Mara's cuffs and shackles, allowing her to break free.

I felt instant relief, instant hope.

This was everything I've wanted; I couldn't begin to imagine how Mara and Ezra felt.

*Now we just need to get the hell away from this cabin.*

Mara was useless, in the nicest way possible.

I understood why she wasn't able to do much, but it was difficult to escape.

She couldn't walk because she was too weak or *drugged.*

She couldn't really talk because she was exhausted or *drugged.*

And she couldn't see shit, because she couldn't even open her eyes from exhaustion, or from being *drugged.*

I pushed my arms under her armpits like I did to Ezra, and counted, "One…two…three!"

I stood her up, but she was unstable.

*We just had to get her to the car.*

But it was too late.

Graves and Dennis were here; the squeal of their brakes gave it away, and it was only a matter of time before they made their way into the house from the driveway.

They may not suspect anything now, but they sure will as soon as they turn the corner to the hallway.

I gave Mara a glass of water in hopes it might sober her up; she chugged it all, yet she remained unable to function.

"Mara, do you hear me?"

She nodded.

"We have to go; you need to focus."

She took a deep breath, a big gulp, peeped her eyes open just enough to see, then answered: "I can do this."

I tried to lift the window, but no luck… locked, of course.

"Ezra, are your windows locked?"

He nodded his head in a 'yes' motion.

We were *trapped.*

"What about the bathroom?"

"I'm not sure, let me check."

I checked the driveway from the tiny view the window had.

Dennis and Graves were still talking… for now.

"Jordy, it's unlocked, but it's small."

"It'll work."

I looked at Mara, "Mara, are you ready to get out of here?"

He smirked and replied, "Yes."

I helped her get up the same way as before; she was a tad sturdier.

We slowly walked to the bathroom, Ezra following behind and closing the door.

"Jordy, we have a problem."

"What?"

"There's not a lock on this door. One of Graves' controlling things."

"Shit. Umm…" I thought for a split second, "... Lean against it, listen for anyone coming."

But just as those words left my mouth, the front door slammed shut, and boisterous voices followed.

Ezra and I exchanged a look of fright, and I began to panic.

"Alright, Mara, we gotta go, now. Put your foot up here." I whispered and continued to instruct her on how to climb out the window.

The thuds of feet began to echo down the hall... *too close.*

It was officially time for the unavoidable... fighting *Graves* and *Dennis*.

The doors outside the bathroom creaked open, the thuds grew louder, then paused... right out front of the restroom.

I shoved Mara's back half of her body out the window and hopped in the tub, quietly pulling the shower curtain.

Graves kicked the door open, nearly making it fall off its hinges.

He was close enough to smell.

He was just through that sheer curtain.

This fight seemed *inevitable*.

"Ezra. What do you think you're doing?"

"What? What do you mean?"

"Don't play dumb with me. WHAT DID YOU DO?!"

"Nothing, I swear."

"You're out of your chains, and Mara is gone!"

"Dennis let me out of my chains before he left. I don't know anything about Mara. Maybe he let her go. He seemed awfully generous this morning."

"Hmmm…."

The pause didn't seem reassuring; he didn't believe Ezra's lie.

A loud noise rang out, making me jump.

Mara squealed, but it was muffled.

I hoped Graves didn't hear through the commotion.

I peeked through the crack between the wall and the curtain to see Ezra on the ground.

Bloody forehead and hair, barely conscious, unstable.

That commotion was from Graves… beating the life out of Ezra.

Out of his *own brother.*

Out of *my lover.*

All the techniques I had learned while boxing over the past few months began flooding my mind.

Everything I had done this past year has led up to this moment, and then I did what anyone else would have done... jumped out from behind the curtain and began to attack Graves.

It was challenging because my adrenaline was high and the space was limited.

Although it wasn't the ideal location to be fighting my first battle, and with Graves at that, it was the harsh reality that I faced.

I began throwing punches and kicks one after another, keeping everything synchronized and smooth.

I was making solid contact and a solid impact on Graves.

These were the two most important things I was taught in boxing: solid contact, solid impact.

However, one thing that nobody can ever change is the *size* of their opponent.

And unfortunately, Graves was bigger, stronger, and filled with way more muscle.

I didn't even compare to him.

He threw two punches to my gut and a forceful kick, sending me back into the tub, and accidentally pulling the curtain down with me.

His anger was visible on his face.

He had a frown, grinding his teeth, with a red face and accompanying red ears.

And right before he went to get me, a deafening gunshot rang out milliseconds before his blood splattered all across the walls.

Painting the once light blue walls a deep red.

His knees crumbled to the ground.

The truck that was just in the driveway sped away.

*Dennis.*

"Mara, let's go. Ezra pull the car around." I demanded as I handed him the keys to the Camry.

And while Mara and I walked over the unrecognizable body to exit, there was a wave of new beginnings that washed over me.

He was gone.

Mara was saved.

Ezra was a good man.

And this was all finally over.

Sirens wailed in the distance as we entered the outside; they were coming to help us.

Instead of speeding away recklessly, I chose to sit down on the weathered wooden steps of the front porch, allowing the warmth of the fading sunlight to wash over me.

Mara settled beside me; her presence was a comforting anchor after all the chaos.

Ezra sat in the car with a look of confusion etched on his face as he attempted to piece together the situation in his mind.

But after a moment, he stepped forward and joined me on the other side, providing comfort and support, too.

I reached for Mara's hand.

I leaned my head on Ezra's shoulder.

Then, I closed my eyes for a moment, trying to gather my thoughts.

"I'm sorry it took me so long to save you guys," I murmured, my voice trembling as I fought back tears.

The weight of my emotions pressed heavily on my chest, but a small spark of hope flickered within me, brightening the darkness I had felt for so long, just a little.

# *Epilogue*

It's been a while since I last thought about the details of what happened to us in the Great Smoky Mountains.

It's hard to think about it, especially the older I get, and the more time passes.

Because that means that's how long Dennis Martin has been running.

He's still free, out there, and if he's anything like Graves, he's on the hunt... for *us*.

\* \* \*

Mara has continued to live with her parents ever since their reunion.

It's a beautiful story, because her parents were truly heartbroken without her… all to finally have her back.

I miss her, though, every single day.

It's not the same without talking to her all the time.

She deleted all her social media and ditched her phone right after she returned home, so I don't even have a way to contact her.

But I still write letters to her once a month.

I never hear anything back, but that's okay.

It's truly about her reading the letter.

Ezra and I have continued to live together and bought a beautiful mountain home in Breckenridge, Colorado.

We're far from Mara and my home in Kentucky, but we had to get away.

Far away, so his dad couldn't find us.

It breaks my heart that Mara isn't here with us, but I understand she wanted to soak in that precious time that can never be made up.

Ezra and I live a happy, average, mountain life now.

And we *love* it.

It is everything I've ever dreamt of and more.

And he is the most amazing, respectful, caring, and handsome man I've ever met.

But even though life is good, and has been for going on three years now... we're still *not* safe.

As long as Dennis remains hidden in the shadows,

we are *not* safe.

www.ingramcontent.com/pod-product-compliance
Lightning Source LLC
Chambersburg PA
CBHW061248170626
46809CB00007B/2906